The Wish Fairy

Too Many Cats!

ALSO BY LISA ANN SCOTT

The Wish Fairy

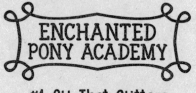

ENCHANTED PONY ACADEMY

The Wish Fairy

Too Many Cats!

Lisa Ann Scott

illustrated by
Heather Burns

SCHOLASTIC INC.

Text copyright © 2018 by Lisa Ann Scott
Illustrations by Heather Burns, © 2018 Scholastic Inc.

ISBN 978-1-338-12097-4

10 9 8 7 6 5 4 3 2 1   18 19 20 21 22

Printed in the U.S.A.   40

First printing 2018

Book design by Yaffa Jaskoll

To my awesome agent,
Jennifer Unter, for finding such a
magical home for my books.

Chapter 1

Friday after school, Brooke burst out the door into her backyard and found her cat lounging in a sunbeam. "Hey, Patches, race you to the meadow!"

Patches yawned and rolled over.

Brooke nudged the furry lump with her toe. "Let's explore!" Brooke always found interesting treasures in the meadow: empty birds' nests, creepy praying mantises, sparkly rocks. "Come on! You can chase mice and bugs!"

Patches twitched her whiskers and reluctantly got to her feet.

Brooke ran across the lawn until she reached the big field of flowers and tall grass. She could still see her house, but she was far enough away that it felt like an adventure.

Brooke twirled in a circle and tumbled onto the ground, admiring the puffy clouds chugging across the sky. She could see her tree house by the creek at the edge of the forest. A rainbow of flower heads bobbed in the breeze. Being out here always felt magical. "One more month of fourth grade, then we can play all summer long," she said to the cat.

With a loud purr, Patches curled up beside her for another nap.

"You are the best cat in the world." Brooke stroked Patches' long, silky fur. Then she stood and plucked a handful of flowers. "I'll weave crowns for us and for Izzy, too. She'll be here soon."

Since Brooke's best friend, Izzy, didn't have a pet, Brooke shared Patches when Izzy visited. They both loved cats more than any other animal. Lots of people thought dogs were the most loyal pet, but Brooke knew Patches would always be by her side.

Brooke sat down with the flowers in her lap. She began tying dandelion and daisy stems together, humming as she worked.

Patches' ears perked up, then she sprang to her feet. With a fast, powerful paw she batted at something fluttering in the air, pinning it to the ground.

Brooke dropped her crown. "Bad kitty! Did you catch another dragonfly?" Brooke leaned over and carefully removed Patches' paw off her prey. "We *like* dragonflies. I hope you didn't hurt it."

The creature lay sprawled on the ground, its wings trembling. It didn't look like any dragonfly she'd ever seen before. Brooke scooped it up in her hand—then nearly dropped it. Her mouth opened and closed a few times before she could whisper, "You're not a dragonfly!"

A tiny girl with wings quivered in Brooke's hand. "Goodness, no! I'm not a dragonfly, *blech*! I'm a fairy."

Brooke blinked. And blinked again. She was speechless.

The fairy snapped her fingers. "Hello? Can you see me? Have I disappeared? I thought I hadn't mastered that trick yet." The fairy slowly stood up on Brooke's palm. She was only a few inches tall. She was extraordinary, with pale blue skin, darker blue hair, and bright green eyes. Dirt covered her beautiful yellow dress, and her iridescent wings were bent.

Brooke cleared her throat. "I . . . I . . . can see you. I just can't believe I'm holding a real, live fairy."

Frowning, the fairy smoothed out her wings. "Barely alive, thanks to that hideous creature."

"I'm so sorry. Patches didn't mean any harm. I'm sure she didn't know you were a fairy. And she's not hideous. Cats are the best animals in the world. They're loyal and kind. They're often misunderstood."

The fairy wrinkled her nose. "They're beasts who eat us as snacks."

"Us?" Brooke's eyebrows shot up. "There are more of you?"

"Of course. We live deep in the forest in Fairvana. Most fairies are too frightened to visit your world." The fairy paced across the palm of Brooke's hand. "But I'm not afraid. I know more about humans than any fairy in

school. You're very interesting creatures. I'm not scared of you at all. That's why my . . . friends . . . Jasmine and Starla dared me to fetch a strand of human hair. It makes excellent rope, you know. I was just about to pull one out of your head when this *monster* tried to kill me."

Patches innocently blinked at the fairy.

"Bad kitty," Brooke scolded again. Then to the fairy she said, "I'm so sorry. What is your name?"

"Calla."

"I'm Brooke. And I'll be happy to give you a strand of my hair to show your friends."

"Thank you, but I won't be returning home anytime soon." Calla fluttered up in the air off Brooke's hand, then gently landed back in her palm. "Good. I don't think my wings are broken."

"Then why can't you fly back home?" Brooke asked.

Calla crossed her arms and stuck her nose in the air. "Because first, I owe you seven wishes for saving my life."

Chapter 2

Brooke's jaw dropped. "Are you serious? I get to make seven wishes? Yahoo!" Brooke jumped in the air, knocking Calla out of her hand. "Whoops!"

Calla tumbled toward the ground, nearly crashing, until she fluttered her wings and swooped up.

Patches watched closely, her tail tick-tocking back and forth.

"I fear I'm rather woozy." Calla swiped her forehead with the back of her hand. "May I sit on your shoulder?"

"Of course." Brooke brushed her hair behind her back to clear a space, then carefully sat back down in the grass. "Now about those wishes. You're not teasing me?"

"Sadly, no." Calla sighed. "We fairies know the rules: seven wishes for a life spared. The fairy folk will tease me forever for getting caught. And the king—oh, he's going to be so mad. We're not supposed to reveal ourselves to humans."

"That's okay. I don't have to make any wishes." Brooke craned her neck so she could see the lovely creature on her shoulder. "You can just go home if it keeps you from getting in trouble. I don't mind."

Calla flew down and stood on Brooke's leg. She crossed her arms, staring at Brooke. "Interesting."

"What?" Brooke asked.

"I read that humans were horrible and selfish. But your offer was very kind."

Brooke's eyes widened. "I mean it. I don't want to cause problems for you."

"I cannot leave. It is the law of our land. I must grant your wishes. And I must stay with you until I do. Besides, perhaps spending time with you will earn me extra credit in my Understanding Humans class. Honestly, it's rather exciting to be here, conversing with a real human. Even if you *are* known to be loud and rude." Calla flew off Brooke's leg and twirled in the air. "I want to try your food, and see the castles in which you live and the horse carriages in which you travel! Show me everything!"

Brooke laughed. "Of course. But we don't use horse carriages. Your books must be old."

Calla waved her hand, and a tiny journal and quill appeared in front of her. "Then I must take notes."

"Be sure to add that we're not mean," Brooke said.

Calla jotted a few notes in the book. "That remains to be proven. Now, no more dilly-dallying. Make a wish."

Brooke blinked. "Right now?"

"Yes! You must have something to wish for?"

Brooke nodded, thinking. "Can I wish for anything?"

The fairy sighed. "Not anything. Of course there are rules. I can't bring people back to life. You can't go backward or forward in time. No making anyone fall in love, or do something against their will. If you make such a wish and it doesn't come true, then it's a wasted wish."

"But I can wish for anything else?" Brooke's mind spun with ideas.

"Yes, you may. But the wishes expire in a fortnight. You can't detain me for years waiting to make just the right wish. Of course, from what I hear, most people cast theirs quickly and foolishly." Calla smirked.

Brooke shook her head, her dark curls flying. "I won't. I'll make good wishes. I'm going to think long and hard about each one."

"Please do. You have to be careful what you wish for."

"What do you mean?"

Calla flew up off Brooke's leg and smiled. "Things don't always work out as planned. There's a whole book about it." She landed on top of a big rock, far from Patches' reach.

"That won't happen to me. I'm going to choose something incredible. I'm going to make the most wonderful wish in the world." Brooke paced across the meadow, picking flowers and popping off the blossoms while she thought of all the things she could wish for. A new bike? A bigger bedroom? Oh, there were so many things she wanted. She snapped her fingers. "I know the perfect wish!"

Calla held up her tiny hand. "If you're thinking about wishing for more wishes, you cannot."

Brooke's smile fell. "How did you know? Can you read my mind?"

Calla laughed. "Of course not. I've just been told that's what most humans want first." Bugs and butterflies swarmed above Calla and she led them in a dance around the rock.

Brooke thought some more about her favorite things: candies and snacks, trips to the amusement park. Nothing seemed worthy of a wish from a fairy. And she had seven of them to make? Would she be able to come up with seven perfect things to wish for?

"Well? Can't you think of anything you want?" Calla asked.

"I'm trying to choose something amazing. But I'm not sure what." Brooke looked up at the sky, like she might find the answer there.

"What do you love more than anything in the world?" Calla placed different flower blossoms on her head like hats.

Besides her family and Izzy, Brooke really loved ice cream and bike rides and . . . "Cats!" She snapped her fingers. "I want more cats!"

"*Eek!*" Calla zoomed into the air, then landed on top of Brooke's head, losing her flower hat. "More of those creatures that tried to kill me?"

Brooke laughed. "I won't let them hurt you. You can hide in my pocket." She held open the pocket of her favorite denim vest, which she wore over a T-shirt. It was handy for collecting treasures. "It's the perfect size for you."

Calla floated down on graceful wings and tucked herself in a pocket. "It's quite nice in here. Thank you very much. Now, are you sure that's what you want to wish for? More cats?" Calla shivered.

"Yes."

But what would her mother say? Maybe she didn't have to know. Maybe Brooke could keep it a secret. Besides, what could be better than a bunch of beautiful, fluffy, sweet cats?

"Very well," said Calla. "But here's a tip. You need to be specific with your wishes. How many cats? What kind? Where do you want them to show up?"

Brooke thought about it and shrugged. "One hundred. That's a good number. One hundred beautiful cats, right here in the meadow. Patches loves it and they will, too." Plus, her mother wouldn't know about her new pets. She rarely came back here.

"You want one hundred cats to appear in the meadow? Then make it official and wish for it."

"Yes. Calla, I wish for one hundred cats to live in my meadow."

Calla nodded and rubbed her hands together. A spray of glitter shot through the air, so bright that Brooke had to close her eyes. When she opened them, the field was filled with cats sitting and staring at her.

Chapter 3

Oh my gosh!" Brooke yelped. "Look at them all." There were old cats, young cats, fuzzy cats, and sleek cats. Cats of all colors. Cats of all sizes. "They're so cute! They're amazing! Thank you, Calla, thank you!"

"Just keep them away from me." Calla hunkered down in the pocket as Brooke scooped two kitties into her arms.

A few cats raced after bugs, and others leapt around the field. Tails flicked and whiskers twitched. Meows and yowls filled the air.

Patches flattened her ears and ran toward the house.

"Patches, come back!" Brooke sighed as her cat disappeared. "Guess she's going to have to get used to so many new friends."

Brooke examined the two kitties she held. "How am I going to name you all?" In her right arm was a pure black cat. "You're Midnight." She released him and turned to the Siamese kitty in her left arm. "And you are Sapphire."

She gave Sapphire a few pats, then set her down. Brooke surveyed the field, taking in all the different kinds of cats: calico, Persian, tabby, several more Siamese, pure white cats, gray cats, and tuxedo cats. She could cuddle with them all day.

Then she spotted Izzy. Her best friend's eyes were wide and her mouth formed a tiny O.

"Oh my gosh, look at all these cats!" Izzy dropped her backpack on the ground.

"Hi! Things are so crazy I didn't notice you got here," Brooke said.

"I can't believe this!" Izzy exclaimed, running in circles. "It's like kitty heaven. I've never seen so many. There must be, like, a hundred cats here."

"One hundred exactly!" Brooke grabbed Izzy's hands and squealed. "Isn't it amazing?"

Izzy squealed, too, jumping in place. "Totally amazing! I can't—I don't—Wow—This is like—" Izzy was talking faster and faster, like she did sometimes.

"Take a few deep breaths," Brooke said. "Like your mom tells you—stop and smell a rose?"

Izzy nodded, closed her eyes, and drew in a few deep breaths. "Okay, that's better. So, wow, where did they all come from?" Izzy knelt down and stroked a Himalayan cat rubbing against her leg.

Brooke bit her lip. "I don't think you'd believe me if I told you."

"Of course I would, we're best friends," Izzy said.

"Well, I don't know if I *can* tell you."

A mumbled voice came from Brooke's pocket.

"What?" Brooke asked.

Calla stuck her head out of the pocket. "Phew, it's hot in there. I said, you can tell her if you want to."

Izzy stumbled backward and fell on her butt, almost landing on a big tabby. She pointed at Brooke. "What is that in your pocket?"

"Excuse me? I'm not a what, I'm a who." Calla flew out of Brooke's pocket and fluttered in front of Izzy.

"This is Calla. She's a fairy." Brooke pulled Izzy up off the ground. "Can you believe it? Patches caught her and I saved her life."

"So I have to grant her seven wishes," Calla explained, hopping from flower to flower.

"Oh." Izzy gulped. "A fairy. Fairies are real. And they grant wishes." She gulped again, looking dazed.

"Only if you save one," Calla corrected.

"This is the strangest dream." Izzy slowly shook her head. "Wait until I tell Brooke."

"I'm right here, and it's not a dream." Brooke lightly pinched Izzy's arm, making her flinch. "I wished for one hundred cats, and I've got six wishes left."

Izzy shrugged and blew out a long breath. "Okay then. One hundred cats. From Calla. The fairy. Not a bad wish. And I thought having a long weekend with no homework was exciting."

"I know! This is amazing. Want to help me name them all?" Brooke asked.

Izzy unzipped her backpack. "I brought a notebook with a schedule for our sleepover, but we can use it to keep track of cat names, too."

"Let's record what they look like, and then write down their names," Brooke suggested.

Izzy held up her hand for a high five and the two girls slapped hands.

"Stop! Don't hit each other," Calla hollered. "I thought you were friends."

Brooke laughed. "We are. That's a way to celebrate, to show we're excited."

Calla scrunched her eyebrows together. "Humans are strange, indeed. I'll have to jot that down in my journal, too. Now, may I return to your pocket please? That big striped beast over there is licking its lips."

Brooke held open her pocket and Calla slid in.

"Let's name that black one Grover."

Izzy made a note in her book.

"That yellowish one can be Sweetie," Brooke said. "And how about Blossom for that all-white one?"

"Perfect! They're all so cute. Which

one's your favorite?" Izzy asked. "Besides Patches, of course."

"I don't know! It's too hard to pick," Brooke said.

"Aww, look at that cute orange tabby!" Izzy handed the notebook to Brooke and picked up a silky cat with big green eyes. "It's purring!"

"It likes you," Brooke said.

"You need a special name." Izzy kissed the kitty's head.

"Killer?" Calla suggested from her hiding spot.

Izzy laughed. "No—Pumpkin!"

Pumpkin nuzzled against Izzy's cheek.

Brooke added the name to the list.

An hour and fifty cat names later, they were running out of ideas.

"We can choose the rest tomorrow," Brooke said.

"Come on, let's play with them!" Izzy set down Pumpkin and ran through the field. Kitties trotted and pounced behind her. Pumpkin stayed by her side.

Brooke flicked flower heads into the air, and cats bounded through the grass looking for them.

Brooke and Izzy ran to the big flat rock in the middle of the field and climbed on top of it. Several cats jumped up with them, and the girls took turns petting them.

Cats rolled on their backs and the girls

scratched dozens of bellies until the fur balls fell asleep.

After naptime, the girls chased a pack of them round and round the meadow. The cats ran through the hollow log that Brooke and Izzy used for hiding treasures. The animals climbed on top of the old rock wall at the back of the meadow and scratched at trees by the stream.

Brooke put her hands on her hips. "It's really hard keeping an eye on so many cats."

Breathless, Izzy nodded.

Soon, the sweet meows were sounding more like angry, desperate yowls. Cats rubbed against the girls' legs, while others walked in circles, whining.

"They're probably hungry." Izzy wobbled amidst the crush of cats.

"And thirsty," Brooke added.

"I am, too!" Calla hollered from the pocket.

"What do fairies eat?" Brooke asked.

Calla popped her head out and closed her eyes, dreamily. "Flower petals and nectar. Honey is always delightful. I would love to be on the food collection crew at home. I'm certain they sneak the best treats for themselves."

"We'll get you some great food," Izzy said.

"Want to camp outside tonight so we can watch over the cats?" Brooke asked her.

"Yes!" shouted Izzy while Calla cried, "Nooo!"

Chapter 4

Brooke charged into the kitchen and gathered all the sweets she could find into a sandwich bag: chocolate chips, sugar cubes, and jelly beans. She made up another bag of snacks for her and Izzy with carrots, cashews, and cheese sticks. Izzy wasn't supposed to eat a lot of sugar, so Brooke always made sure to have healthy snacks at home for her that they both could share.

Finally she called across the house,

"We're going to the store to get some snacks for our sleepover, okay, Mom?" Brooke didn't have to mention that the snacks were for dozens of cats.

"I want snacks, too!" Calla whispered from Brooke's pocket.

"Shh!" Brooke dropped a chocolate chip into her vest pocket.

"That's fine," her mom called.

It wasn't far. They just had to ride down the street, take a left, and go two blocks to get to the general store. Brooke and Izzy loved biking into their tiny town, circling the roundabout again and again.

"Thanks!" Brooke said.

Calla popped her head out of the pocket.

"What is this divine sustenance? I've never tasted such a thing."

"It's a chocolate chip!" Brooke looked down and giggled. Calla's face was covered in chocolate.

"Let's get the money in my piggy bank." Brooke dashed upstairs and emptied the

bank onto her bed. Counting the coins and bills, she frowned. "I only have eighteen dollars and some change. I don't know if that'll be enough to get food for all those cats."

"You could wish for food," Izzy offered.

Brooke shook her head. "Wishes can't fix everything. And I don't want to waste a wish on that. We'll figure something out."

Izzy nodded. "You're right."

"What is this?" Calla hovered over Brooke's dollhouse. "Who lives in this glorious home? The cat?" She wrinkled her nose.

Brooke giggled. "No one lives there. That's a pretend house, for my dolls."

"It's just the right size for you, Calla," said Izzy.

Calla walked through the house,

inspecting the furniture. "Amazing!" She reached up and grabbed the chandelier, swinging back and forth. "Whee!"

"That's not a swing!" Brooke said, laughing.

"Are you sure?"

"Yes, it's a chandelier. For light."

Calla let go and fluttered up the stairs. "Oh, the slumber chamber!" She threw herself onto the bed and sprawled out on top of it. "I want to sleep here tonight."

"We're camping outside."

"That's fine, I'll stay in here." Calla snuggled under the covers.

"You can't, my mom might discover you!" Brooke shook her head. "Who knows what she'd do if she spotted you. And you said you're not supposed to reveal yourself to humans."

Calla frowned, then stood and peered into a tiny mirror. "Oh! What a mess. Look at my beautiful gown. It's ruined."

"You can have one of my doll's dresses. They're in that golden wardrobe in the corner," Brooke said.

Calla raced to the fancy cupboard. She gasped as she opened it. "These are glorious!" She held one up, spinning in a circle. "This one is far more beautiful than any gown in Fairvana. If I can't stay inside, might I bring some of those magnificent treasures outside?"

"Sure," Brooke said. "I don't play with this stuff much anymore."

"I'll take this, and this and this . . ." Calla

tossed tiny pillows and dresses and dishes and candlesticks toward the girls.

"Slow down!" Izzy said, laughing.

Brooke piled all the goodies in a box.

Then Calla started pushing the bed toward them. "And I'll be needing this, too. Normally I sleep on a milkweed mattress. This will be a lovely change."

Calla quickly changed into a beautiful new gown. "The human world is more wonderful than I imagined!"

Chapter 5

Brooke and Izzy hopped on their bikes. They rode to the store while Calla shrieked, "Woo hoo! Faster!"

Izzy and Brooke parked their bikes in front of the corner store and walked inside toward the pet section. Calla crouched in the shirt pocket.

Brooke grabbed a big bag of dry cat food. "We have enough money for two bags."

Izzy picked up a big jar of catnip. "Let's make them some toys, too."

"Great idea," Brooke said.

"Do we have time to go to the library?" Izzy asked. "We could take out some books on caring for cats."

"Perfect!" Brooke said.

After paying for the food and stashing it in their bike baskets, they pedaled past the gazebo in the town park. As always, the girls honked their bike horns when they passed the geese in the pond. The geese honked back and they both laughed.

Calla stuck her head out of the shirt

pocket, inhaling the sweet smells of the bakery as they pedaled by. "What wonderful delights you have in this world."

"Smells like cinnamon buns," Brooke said.

"Magnificent!" Calla said.

They parked in front of the library, and Izzy warned, "Calla, you have to be quiet in the library."

"Stay hidden in my pocket for now," Brooke told her.

Calla grumbled but huddled in the pocket as they walked inside.

"Hi Mrs. Nelson, where are the pet books?" Izzy asked the librarian.

"Hello, girls. They're in the back right corner."

"Thanks!" Izzy dashed toward the area.

"Slow down!" Brooke warned.

"Sorry, I'm just excited."

"I know," Brooke said. "Me too. We have a lot to learn about taking care of so many cats."

Once they found the aisle and started browsing the books, Calla flew out of Brooke's pocket. She spun in circles, taking it all in. "I never knew there were this many books in the world! How amazing!"

"And this is just one library!" Izzy said.

"My word!" Calla zoomed along the row reading all the titles, while Brooke grabbed an armful of cat books.

As they checked out, Brooke noticed a tin collection can that read, "Help the Library Fund." She reached in her pocket and dropped in the change she had left from the store.

"Thank you, dear," the librarian said. "Our budget is in terrible trouble. We couldn't even buy new books this year."

"I'm so sorry," Brooke said. "I wish I could do more."

"Is that an official wish?" Calla whispered.

Brooke clasped her hand over the pocket.

"I hope you get enough money," Brooke said.

"That's very kind of you," Mrs. Nelson said. "Thank you for your donation." She passed the books back to the girls. "Enjoy your reading. You must really like cats. Do you have one?"

"I do. Quite a few actually," Brooke said, trying not to giggle.

"Well, good luck. Cats can be a lot of work. I have several myself." She picked up a picture frame and showed it to them. Five cats were lined up on a couch. "That little golden one on the end got out last night. That's Taffy. I'll have to look for her when I get home."

"Hope you find her!" Izzy said.

They waved good-bye and headed out the door, stuffing the books in their baskets next to the cat food.

Calla popped out of Brooke's pocket. "Is that your next wish? More money for the library?"

"No, it's just a saying, 'Wishing you could

do something.' It means you really want to do something, but probably can't. I'd like to help the library, but I'm not sure what's going to be my next wish."

"Be cautious with that phrase. You don't want to make an accidental wish," Calla said.

Brooke nodded, and climbed on her bike.

"I can't believe they just let you take all those books!" Calla said.

"That's how libraries work. You can borrow them and bring them back. Don't you have a library?" Izzy asked.

"No. Our books must stay at school. How amazing to be able to choose from them all. Wait until I tell everyone in Fairvana."

As Brooke pedaled her bike home, she

thought about how wonderful a library really was. She could read any book she wanted—for free. It was amazing.

Once they got to Brooke's house, they gathered their things, including the box of dollhouse items, to spend the night outside. Then they set up camp in the meadow and

scattered dishes of food for the cats. The hungry animals swarmed around the dishes, nudging each other out of the way. Dozens of tails waved in the air like furry flags.

Calla zoomed out of Brooke's pocket, hovering well out of reach. "Just so there's no mistaking me for a snack. I'm sure I look delectable."

Laughing, Brooke set out a few bowls and poured water into them. "I didn't realize how much work it would be taking care of one hundred cats."

"I know," Izzy said.

In minutes, the food and water was gone.

Brooke gulped. "We only have one bag left."

"I can get money from my piggy bank tomorrow to buy more," Izzy offered.

"Thanks, Izzy. You're a great friend." Brooke wrapped one arm around Izzy in a friendly hug.

Just then, Calla zoomed between them. "We have a very big problem."

Chapter 6

Calla crawled onto Brooke's shoulder, hiding under her hair.

Brooke giggled. "That tickles!"

"What's wrong?" Izzy asked.

"I just spotted two fairies. They're probably looking for me," Calla said.

Izzy's eyes bulged. "Where are they?"

"They're perched in that bush near your tent," Calla said. "They were probably sent to find me."

"Shouldn't you let them know you're fine?" Brooke asked.

"But then they'll know I was discovered by humans. How embarrassing!"

Brooke put her hands on her hips. "Don't worry. We'll handle this."

Brooke walked over to the small green bush not far from their tent. Izzy followed. They knelt in front of it.

"I know I saw something moving around in here," Brooke said.

"Me too," Izzy said. She pointed to what looked like a shimmering leaf. "What's that?"

"That's a fairy!" Brooke said.

"And there's another one!" Izzy parted the branches, exposing the two small fairies crouched inside.

"Humans!" shouted a tiny fairy with gold hair.

"Ack! Starla, this is all your fault," a tiny pink-haired fairy yelled. "They probably noticed your shiny blue gown. I told you not to wear that one."

The golden-haired fairy in the blue dress stood on the branch and wagged a finger at her friend. "And I told *you* not to get so *close*, Jasmine."

As the two fairies fought, Calla flew from behind Brooke's back. "It's my fault!" she cried. "You came looking for me, didn't you?"

"You're alive?" Starla asked. "The humans didn't eat you?"

"Of course not. I saved her from my cat," Brooke said.

Starla and Jasmine gasped.

"Yes, yes, now I owe her seven wishes."
Calla hung her head. "So go back and tell the
king I'll return in a fortnight ... if one of
these cats doesn't kill me first."

The two fairies started laughing in a
mean way.

"Why are you laughing at your friend?"

Izzy asked. "That's not very nice. You should be grateful she's alive."

"You think Calla is our *friend*?" Starla laughed even harder.

"You're not very kind," Brooke said. "And it's your fault my cat caught her. It was your idea for her to steal some of my hair."

Jasmine rolled her eyes. "We didn't think she'd actually find a human. We were trying to keep her away from us. She can be quite tiresome."

Calla's lower lip trembled.

"And you're quite mean," Izzy said.

"How rude," Starla said.

"What do you expect, they're humans," Jasmine said.

"Surprisingly, these humans aren't so horrible after all," Calla said.

Brooke scooped Calla into her hand and held her against her chest. "We're happy to have Calla here."

"Yeah, only because she's granting your wishes," Jasmine said.

"That's not why," Brooke said. "We like Calla."

Izzy shook the bush. "If you're going to keep being nasty, then leave."

"Humans, yuck," Starla said.

"They really are atrocious," Jasmine added.

The fairies whizzed off into the sky, and Calla flew onto a rock, sat down, and rested her chin in the palm of her hand. "I'm sorry I lied when I said my friends dared me to get a strand of hair. I don't have friends. I'm not very popular."

Izzy shrugged. "We're not the most popular kids in school, either. We sit alone at lunch."

Brooke put her arm around Izzy and squeezed. "But we've got each other. There must be nicer fairies in Fairvana than those two."

"None that want to be friends with me." Calla sighed. "And now when I return after being discovered by humans, I'll be the laughingstock of my village."

"You don't know that," Izzy said. "If they're so afraid of us, maybe they'll think you're brave. They might want to hear your stories."

Calla raised her head. "You think? Maybe you're right. Perhaps everyone will want to be my friend when I return, to hear of my adventures."

Brooke smiled. "I'm sure of it."

"You two are so lucky to be best friends," Calla said. "If I had a wish, it would be for a best friend."

"You'll have a best friend someday," Izzy said. "I just know it."

"But I have no practice being a friend."

"Well, it's always nice to be helpful to your friends. Maybe you can help us make some cat toys, Calla?" Brooke asked.

Calla did a few loop-de-loops in the air. "Certainly!"

Chapter 7

The two girls and the fairy sat together in the meadow and got to work. They placed scoops of catnip onto scraps of material from Brooke's craft bin. Brooke and Izzy pinched the fabric closed while Calla flew around with a piece of yarn, tying it together.

Brooke tossed one of the pouches to the nearest cat, laughing as he snatched it in his teeth and ran off. She threw another one into the field, and several kitties rushed for it, pouncing over each other for a chance to bat around the small toy.

Izzy laughed. "We need to make more."

They spent the next two hours putting together pouches. "Wow, all that work and we only have thirty," Brooke said.

"We'll make more tomorrow." Izzy set aside her material.

Brooke yawned and stretched. "I'm exhausted. It's been a crazy day."

"I'll say," Calla agreed. "I still can't believe I'm living in the human world."

"I'm sure you'll make new friends if you bring some chocolate chips back to Fairvana!" Brooke said.

"That's a good idea," Calla said as she nibbled one.

Brooke and Izzy ate the sandwiches they'd made for dinner, then settled into the tent, snuggling up in their sleeping bags. They each grabbed a library book and clicked on their flashlights to read.

But the cats weren't quieting down. A chorus of meows joined the peeping frogs and cooing doves outside.

Izzy sat up. "Why aren't they going to sleep?"

"My book says cats are nocturnal. They like to hunt at night," Brooke said.

"Hunt?" Calla yelped. "Hunt for what?"

One of the cats let out a high-pitched yowl, and several others joined in.

"Mice, little critters," Brooke said.

"You do realize if I die, there are no more

wishes, right? Isn't there somewhere safer to sleep?" Calla asked.

Brooke snapped her fingers. "The tree house!"

They gathered their things and placed them in a basket attached to a rope and pulley at the base of the tree. Then the girls climbed up the ladder to the tree house that

Brooke's grandfather had built for her mother when she was young. Finally, they pulled up the basket.

"Humans sleep in trees!" Calla exclaimed, making a few notes in her journal.

"*Some*times," Izzy said with a laugh.

Brooke lit several lanterns, illuminating the room: the jars of treasures they'd collected over the years with dried seed pods and nuts, fossils from the creek, feathers, and broken eggshells. Two small beds were tucked in along the sides, and trunks held their supplies.

At last they helped Calla set up the bed and furniture they'd brought from Brooke's dollhouse.

Izzy checked her notebook. "Good job! Bedtime is right on schedule. It's almost 9:30."

Brooke peered out the window into the darkness of the forest. "I can't believe *fairies* live right in the forest next to my house."

Tiny blue-green lights winked in the trees. "Look at the fireflies!" Brooke exclaimed. She reached for the binoculars they kept stashed in their adventure trunk. It was filled with all the supplies they needed to explore. She put them up to her eyes and gazed into the forest for a better look.

"Those aren't fireflies. They're wisps," Calla said, fluffing the pillows on her tiny bed.

"What are you talking about?" Izzy asked. "What is a wisp?"

"Ah, I forgot. You know nothing about the forest." Calla fluttered out the window and whistled an elaborate song.

Several blue lights zoomed their way.

"Come on, it's safe," Calla told the creatures.

Tiny, glowing, ghostly shaped creatures

perched on the windowsill. They were smaller than Calla, with impish smiles and big eyes. They giggled, then zoomed around the tree house.

"Oh my gosh," Brooke whispered. "They live in the forest, too?"

"Yes, and they can be quite mischievous, leading many a human astray with their glowing forms," Calla explained.

"I can't believe I've never seen them before." Brooke cocked her head. "But then again, I've never been in the forest."

"Me neither," Izzy said. "I can't believe we've never gone exploring."

"Of course you haven't." Calla laughed. "The woods were cast with a magical spell to keep humans out."

The wisps whirled out of the room, back into the darkness of the trees, while Calla jumped into her doll bed and snuggled under the covers.

"A magical spell?" Brooke whispered. "Are there other magical creatures out there?"

"Of course. But most live near Fairvana, in the fairy realm." Calla yawned.

"How big is your village?" Izzy asked.

"Oh, there are hundreds of fairy families. Everyone has a job. My family collects empty snail shells to carve into cups. Terribly boring. I'd rather sew dresses. Or search for human artifacts." Calla tugged the blanket up to her chin. "What a stressful day. I must get some sleep." Calla was soon snoring.

Izzy laughed. "For someone so tiny, she's quite loud."

"I know. A fairy. I still can't believe it!" With a contented sigh, Brooke curled up on her side and patted around, looking for Patches. Her cat always slept next to her. Then she remembered Patches had run back home. She missed her kitty.

Oh, well. I'll find her tomorrow, Brooke thought, before dozing off.

Chapter 8

Brooke woke to the sound of Izzy's giggles.

"What's so funny?"

Izzy slapped her hand over her mouth and pointed at a furry orange lump curled up next to her. "Pumpkin's sleeping with Calla!"

Sure enough, Calla was on the floor next to her bed, curled up in Pumpkin's tail. Calla tugged the fuzzy orange fur around her more tightly. Her eyes fluttered open. "What

a lovely sleep." She stretched and then screamed. "This cat is trying to kill me!"

"No it's not, it's snuggling with you!" Izzy said.

Calla wriggled her way out of the tail. "It was trying to squeeze me to death with its tail like one of those giant snakes in your world!"

Pumpkin looked up at Calla flying above her and meowed softly.

Izzy scooped Pumpkin into her lap.

"Does that mean Izzy gets seven wishes for saving your life?" Brooke teased.

Izzy laughed. "Pumpkin wouldn't hurt a fly."

"And besides, I escaped the clutches of death on my own." Calla flapped her wings a few times and zipped around the tree house. "I'm hungry. Nearly dying takes a lot out of a fairy."

Brooke sat up and groaned. "I'm so tired. I hardly got any sleep at all."

Izzy rubbed her eyes. "I know. One hundred cats are really noisy, even from up here."

"How funny that Pumpkin was the only one who climbed the tree to sleep with us," Brooke said.

Izzy held Pumpkin tightly with one arm as she climbed down the tree house ladder. Brooke followed, and Calla flew down beside them.

"Can we get another chocolate chip?" Calla turned somersaults in the air. "I'm starving. Famished." She pressed the back of her hand against her forehead.

"Yes, we'll go home for breakfast," Brooke said walking toward her house.

Pointy-eared heads popped up around the meadow. The cats rushed toward them, and Calla zoomed on top of Brooke's head.

Brooke sighed. "They want to eat again."

"I'll get the other bag of food." Izzy ducked into the tent and grabbed the bag.

Together, Brooke and Izzy poured out all the food onto the plates for the crowd of happy cats.

"We're going to need more cat food," Izzy said.

"We'll go to the store later. Let's go down to the creek," Brooke suggested. "Maybe the cats will follow us and get a drink so we won't have to fill their bowls with water again."

Izzy tapped the side of her head. "Smart."

Calla flew overhead as the girls walked toward the creek. Dozens of cats followed.

Calla landed on the opposite side of the creek. "This side is magical. The cats won't come over here."

While Brooke and Izzy petted the cats who eagerly lapped up the cool clear water, Calla gathered a pile of things: acorn tops, maple helicopters, snail shells.

"What are you doing?" Brooke asked.

"Water skating. Watch!" She set two acorn tops on the water and put a foot in each one. In each hand she held a helicopter. Then she started gliding across the water! She waved her arms, and the helicopters helped her go faster. "Whee!"

When she was finished, the fairy sat on the bank and scooped up some water with the snail shell and took a long drink.

"We have a creek like this in Fairvana. Only there are far more magical creatures who live there. Not too many here."

"There are other magical creatures here right now? Besides you?" Izzy asked.

"Of course! They lurk throughout the forest, though few are brave enough to come this close. Come out, come out," Calla said.

A creature as tiny as Calla stepped away from a tree. Her body was covered in bark!

"This is a dryad. What's your name?" Calla asked.

It answered so quietly the girls couldn't hear.

"This is Talina," Calla said.

The tiny wooden being waved her leafy fingers at the girls.

Brooke and Izzy's jaws dropped. "Your world is so incredible!" Brooke said.

Then the cats spotted the creature. They started yowling.

"We better go," Brooke said. "I don't want the cats to chase Talina."

"Plus we need to get more cat food," Izzy said.

The dryad scooted into the forest, and the girls tromped back through the fields toward the house, Calla flying above them.

"*Shh*, my mom is still asleep," Brooke whispered, heading to her room.

Brooke pulled fresh clothes out of her dresser, while Izzy went to the bathroom to change. "Patches?" she called softly. "Where are you, girl?" She peeked under her bed, but there was no sign of her kitty. Brooke bit her lip, worried. Where was Patches hiding?

But there was no time to worry. They needed more cat food. After they stopped at Izzy's and emptied her piggy bank, they rode back to the store and parked outside. As they headed for the door, Brooke froze. There was a flyer in the window of the store that read: MISSING CAT: BUBBLES DISAP-PEARED YESTERDAY. PLEASE HELP US FIND HER! There was a name and address listed, along with a picture of the cat.

"That looks like Fluffy," Izzy said. "Look! There's another missing cat poster on that telephone pole." She dashed over and read it. "'Please call if you've seen Taffy. She went missing yesterday. Reward for return.'" Izzy gulped. "That's Mrs. Nelson's cat—and it looks just like Sweetie!"

Brooke reached into her shirt pocket and carefully pinched the back of Calla's dress between her fingers, pulling the fairy out.

"Calla," she said. "Where exactly did those one hundred cats *come* from?"

Chapter 9

Calla hollered and squirmed in Brooke's grasp. "Let me go!" she shouted.

Brooke released the tiny fairy and Calla bobbed in the air in front of her.

"I don't know where the cats came from. You made a wish and they appeared. You didn't say they had to be cats without owners, so they could've come from anywhere." Calla wagged a finger at Brooke. "I warned you: being specific is an absolute must when making wishes."

Brooke frowned and turned to Izzy. "We've got to return those two cats."

Izzy nodded. "But first we need to get food for the rest."

They bought a bag of food, then grabbed the flyers and hurried home. Calla flew into the tent while Izzy and Brooke searched the field for the missing cats.

Some of the cats were sunning themselves, while others licked and groomed their new furry friends. A few stalked the meadow for prey.

"I don't see either of these cats," Izzy said.

"Taffy?" Brooke called. "Bubbles?"

A golden cat that looked a lot like Mrs. Nelson's Taffy ran toward them. Izzy scooped him up and Brooke held the flyer next to him. "This is the one we named Sweetie. It sure looks like the same cat."

"Good. Now let's find Bubbles so we can return them both," Izzy said.

It took a while, but they finally found Bubbles snoozing behind a big rock. She meowed loudly when Brooke picked her up. "We have a cat carrier in the garage we use to take Patches to the vet. They'll both fit in there and we can set it in the wagon and pull them into town."

"Where is Patches?" Izzy asked.

"She ran back to the house last night. She must be hiding. We'll find her later."

Calla flew between Brooke and Izzy as they walked to town.

"Mrs. Nelson lives up here on Grove Street," Brooke said, reading the flyer.

Calla disappeared into Brooke's pocket while Izzy rang the bell.

Mrs. Nelson looked surprised when

she answered the door. "How can I help you two?"

"I think we found your cat." Brooke slid open the latch on the cat carrier and lifted the kitty out.

Mrs. Nelson clapped her hands together. "Yes! That's my Taffy. Thank you ever so

much. I've been so worried. Where did you find her?"

"In the meadow behind my house."

"She's never gotten loose before. I can't imagine what happened."

Brooke felt her cheeks redden. "Well, she's back now, that's all that matters."

"Please wait a moment so I can give you a reward," Mrs. Nelson said.

Brooke held up a hand. "No, that's not necessary. I would be so upset if my cat was missing. We're happy to bring Taffy back." *Plus it's my fault she disappeared . . .*

"Such kind girls." Mrs. Nelson peered at the wagon. "Is there another cat in there?"

"Yep," Izzy said. "We found that one in the meadow, too."

"How strange," Mrs. Nelson said.

"I know. So . . . have a good day! Bye, Taffy."

Next, they returned Bubbles to a teary-eyed toddler who hugged them both.

"I'm so glad we found their owners," Izzy

said as they walked down the road with the empty cat carrier.

As they passed the store, they noticed a dozen new missing cat posters that had been tacked up.

"Oh, no!" Brooke cried.

Izzy snatched the flyers down and piled them into the wagon. "We've got a long day ahead of us."

Chapter 10

Chasing cats is hard!" Brooke paused to wipe her brow. She and Izzy were searching the meadow for Midnight, who was really named Sprite and was sadly missed by her family, according to the flyer.

Calla sat on the branch of a small bush munching on a sugar cube, occasionally shouting out locations of hidden cats.

"Calla, do you see Patches?" Brooke asked.

"I'd be huddled in your pocket if I did," Calla answered.

Brooke shaded her eyes from the sun and looked back and forth across the field. There was no sign of her white cat with black spots.

"I'm sure she's hiding in the house," Izzy said.

Brooke sighed. "I hope so. I never thought about how my wish would affect her. I thought she'd love all these new friends. I'll give her some treats later to make up for it."

"Hey, treats might help lure some of the missing cats to us! Do you have any inside?" Izzy asked.

"Yes. Maybe that'll help find Patches,

too." Brooke ran inside, with Izzy and Calla close behind.

Brooke's mom was in the kitchen baking cookies. "Whoa, what's the rush?"

"I can't find Patches. Have you seen her?" Brooke closed the sliding glass door behind her.

"No." Her mom waved her hand through the air. "Wait, I think a dragonfly flew in!"

Brooke froze. "No it didn't. There was no dragonfly. Nope." Her eyes swept around the kitchen until she spotted Calla perched on top of the refrigerator.

"I definitely didn't see a dragonfly," Izzy said.

"Hmm. Must've been my imagination," Brooke's mom said.

"We're going to get the cat treats and look for Patches," Brooke said. "You sure you haven't seen her? She ran toward the house last night."

"Sorry, kiddo. No sign of her," Mom said.

Brooke gulped. A field full of cats was great, but not if she lost her own kitty.

Her mom reached into the cupboard right next to the refrigerator where Calla sat. Brooke crossed her fingers, hoping her mom wouldn't spot the fairy.

"Here you go," her mom said, handing her the container of treats. "Good luck. I'm sure she'll turn up."

Brooke let out the breath she'd been holding and took the box. "Thanks."

Brooke and Izzy walked to the door, but

Calla was stranded on top of the refrigerator. There was no way for her to leave without Mom seeing!

"Um, hey, did Patches just run through the living room?" Brooke asked.

"Let me look." Her mom went into the other room, while Calla flew off the refrigerator, scooped up a chocolate chip, and slipped into Brooke's pocket.

"I don't think she's in here," Brooke's mom called from the living room.

"Okay. Thanks for looking. See you later!" Brooke called as she and Izzy hurried outside. "What were you doing? You could've been caught!" she scolded Calla.

"But the chocolate chips were just lying there. I needed one."

"You have to stay hidden!" Izzy said.

"I know, I know," Calla grumbled.

They raced back to the field and shook the box of treats. A group of cats surrounded them, including Sparky and Fitch, two of the missing ones.

Brooke frowned. "Patches usually comes running when she hears the treat box."

Izzy patted her back. "Maybe she's still scared of all these cats. Come on, let's take these two back to their owners."

They walked back to town, calling for Patches the whole way. But there was no sign of her.

Brooke blinked back tears. "Where is she? This is horrible. Now I know how these people feel wondering where their missing pets are. And it's all my fault! I should've never wished for those cats."

"Told you so," Calla sang.

"Shush," Izzy said. "It seemed like a great wish at the time."

Once they returned the kitties, the girls passed by the store again. "More missing cat flyers!" Izzy groaned.

"What are we going to do? It'll take forever to return all these cats, and I still have to look for Patches," Brooke said.

"You have six wishes left," Izzy said. "You could use one."

Brooke pulled open her pocket. "Calla, I think I need your help."

Chapter 11

As they walked back to the meadow, Brooke and Izzy debated which would be the best wish to make: to find Patches or to return all the cats to their owners.

"I think once all the cats are gone, Patches will come back," Izzy said. "Plus, it'll save us the work of returning them all. It's hard, and my arms are all scratched up." She held out her arms, which were covered in jagged pink lines.

"True," Brooke said. They stood at the edge of the meadow. Cats started meowing wildly and charging toward the girls.

"They're hungry again," Izzy said.

"I don't want to waste time scooping out all the food. I just want this to be over," Brooke said. "Okay, Calla. Time for a new wish. I wish you'd return these cats to the people they belong to—now."

"Yay! No more cats!" Calla rubbed her hands together and a bright flash lit up the air.

When the glitter cleared, the cats were gone.

"Wow," Izzy said. "Incredible."

"Patches?" Brooke called. "Come on girl, come on out now."

There was a soft meow behind them.

Brooke spun around and saw a kitty running toward her. A fuzzy, orange kitty. "Pumpkin?" Disappointed, she scooped up the cat and turned to Calla. "I wished for all the cats to be returned to the people they belong to. Why is she still here?"

Calla shrugged. "I guess she doesn't belong to anyone."

"She must be a stray. Maybe you can keep her if you don't find Patches," Izzy said softly.

"No!" Brooke handed the cat to Izzy. "I don't want another cat, I want my cat. I want Patches."

Izzy nuzzled the soft orange kitty. "Then what are you going to do with Pumpkin?"

Brooke's eyes widened. "Maybe your parents will let you keep her!"

Izzy's smile fell. "I've asked for a cat dozens of times, but they always say, 'No, we're too busy, you won't take care of it, blah blah blah.'"

"Could I make a wish for Izzy's parents to let her have a cat?" Brooke asked Calla.

The fairy shook her head. "I can't make someone do something they don't want to."

Izzy sighed and nuzzled Pumpkin under her chin. "Let's look for Patches."

They shook the treats, walked back and forth through the meadow, and called for Patches. But there was no sign of her.

Brooke frowned. "Let's check my house again."

Calla slid into Brooke's pocket before they stepped inside. "Mom? Did Patches come back yet?"

"No, I haven't seen her. The treats didn't work?"

Brooke shook her head.

Her mom spotted the cat in Izzy's arms. "Looks like they attracted someone."

"Yes, this is a stray we found in the field," Brooke said.

"I told you, one cat is enough," her mom said.

"I know," Brooke said. "And I totally agree. Now I just need to find that one perfect, awesome cat."

"We will," Izzy assured her. "Let's go to my house first so I can ask to keep Pumpkin."

"Really?" Brooke asked. "I'll cross my fingers for you."

They went outside and headed down the road toward Izzy's house. "If I can't find Patches, can I make a wish for you to find her, Calla?" Brooke asked.

Calla popped her head out of the pocket.

"Sure, but it might not work if she doesn't want to be found. And it would be three wishes gone. I told you humans use them up fast."

"Just wait a little longer," Izzy said. "She'll definitely come home tonight."

"Okay." Brooke nodded trying to keep her lip from trembling. She followed Izzy into her house.

"Mom?" Izzy called. "Dad?"

"We're in the family room," her mother called.

Izzy took a deep breath and tightened her grip on Pumpkin.

"Stay in my pocket," Brooke warned Calla as they walked into the family room.

"What's that in your arms?" Izzy's father asked.

Izzy sat down, took a deep breath, and started talking quickly. "We found this poor little kitty in the meadow and she doesn't have a home and I named her Pumpkin and she's super soft and fuzzy and sweet and please, please, please let me keep her!"

"Slow down," her mom said.

Izzy petted Pumpkin a few times and took another deep breath. She continued, much calmer this time. "I'll take care of her myself. I'll wake up early to feed her and play with her before school. I'll clean the litter box as soon as I get home *and* before I go to bed. I'll write it all in my schedule."

Izzy's dad smiled. "Sounds like you've put a lot of thought into this."

"And that kitty seems to have a soothing effect on you," her mom said. "Sounds good to me. What do you think?" she asked Izzy's dad.

"Yes." Her dad smiled. "You can keep that adorable cat."

Izzy screamed and rushed over to her parents, snuggling on the couch with them and showing them her kitty.

"Oh! I've got a collar I picked out last year just in case you ever let me get a cat." She ran to her room and returned with a pink leather band that she fastened around Pumpkin's neck.

Brooke blinked back tears. She was happy for her friend. Izzy wanted a cat more than anything. But Brooke was getting more and more worried about her own pet. Where could Patches be? Maybe she was gone forever and Izzy would have to share her cat with Brooke now.

Chapter 12

"What's wrong, Brooke?" Izzy's mom asked.

Brooke sniffed. "My cat is missing. We've been looking everywhere, but I'm really worried she's gone for good. I thought she'd always be by my side." Brooke broke down in tears and Izzy's mom hurried over.

She set her hand on Brooke's shoulder. "Oh, honey. I'm so sorry. I should've called your house. Your cat showed up here last night. I thought she'd go back home, but maybe she's still prowling around our back porch."

Brooke's eyes widened. "Really? Patches was *here*? She's never run off before." She swiped her hand to catch her tears and hurried out the back door. Izzy followed.

And there, in a sunbeam on the patio, was Patches. She looked up at Brooke and meowed.

"Patches!" Brooke plopped onto the ground next to her cat and pulled her onto her lap. "I'm so sorry all those cats scared you off. I don't want any other cat but you!" She kissed and hugged her cat. "Izzy, she must've thought your house was a safe place, since she loves you, too."

Izzy sat next to them holding Pumpkin. She scratched Patches behind the ear. "I love you, too, Patches. And I hope you and Pumpkin can be friends. She's very nice."

The two cats blinked at each other, then Pumpkin meowed and Patches meowed back.

"They like each other!" Brooke said. "The book said when a cat blinks at another cat, they're friends."

"Maybe they'll be best friends like us." Izzy slung her arm around Brooke.

"And what about me?" Calla called from the pocket. "Now I've got to deal with *two* of these creatures. Make sure you tell them to leave me alone!"

"Pumpkin loves you," Izzy said. "Come here."

Calla flew over to Izzy.

"Pet her," Brooke said.

Calla zipped over the cat and brushed her hand along Pumpkin's fur. "She is very soft." Calla hovered behind the kitty's head. "I suppose she can't get me back here." She tucked her legs under the cat's new collar. "This might be a nice way to get around when I'm tired from flying."

Then Patches came over and sniffed Calla.

"Help!"

"Don't worry," Brooke said. "She's just saying hello."

Calla struggled to get out from under Pumpkin's collar as Patches licked the fairy's hair.

"She's eating me! Help, she's eating me!"

Brooke and Izzy laughed.

"She's grooming you," Brooke said. "It means she likes you. She thinks you're part of the family."

Patches nudged Calla with her nose, then rolled onto her back.

Brooke smiled. "She's showing you her most vulnerable part—her belly. She trusts you. She knows you're our friend."

"I'm your friend?" Calla asked quietly.

Izzy laughed. "Of course."

Calla's cheeks turned pink. "Wow. I have two friends."

"Four friends. Us and Pumpkin and Patches," Brooke said.

The cats stared at Calla, but they didn't bat a paw at her.

"See? They're leaving you alone. They like you," Izzy said.

"They're staring at me like I'm a yummy chocolate chip," Calla said.

Brooke laughed. "We won't let anything happen to you."

Calla crossed her arms. "Right, because then you won't have any wishes left."

"We *like* you, Calla. We'll always look after you," Izzy said.

Calla grinned. "You don't want just wishes from me? You really like me!" She held up her hand. "Can you hit me?"

"What?" Brooke asked, confused.

"You know, like you two did earlier when you were celebrating. You hit hands."

"Oh, you mean a high five. Sure!" Izzy gently tapped her pointer finger against Calla's hand. Brooke did the same.

"You've got five wishes left, Brooke," Izzy said. "What's your next wish going to be?"

"I don't know," Brooke said. "I really screwed up that first wish. I almost lost Patches, people were missing their pets for a while, we spent all our money..." Brooke snapped her fingers. "I know the perfect wish! I can't believe it wasn't my first one."

"What is it?" Calla asked.

Brooke grinned. "It's the best wish ever."

"Remember," warned Calla, "be *very specific*. And be careful what you wish for."

"I know, I know. But there's no way anything bad can happen with this wish. Calla, I wish for . . ."

The magic continues . . .

The **Wish Fairy**

#2 The Treasure Trap

Brooke bounced on her toes, excited to make her third wish. A real wish—which was really going to come true, from a real fairy!

The first two had been a bit of a disaster, but this third wish was perfect.

"Only five wishes left," Calla said, zipping around in the air above Brooke and her best friend, Izzy. "Use them wisely."

They sat behind Izzy's house. Brooke petted Patches and thought.

This time, Brooke was going to get things exactly right. She didn't want to hurt anyone with her next wish.

"So, what's it going to be?" Izzy asked.

"It's the perfect wish. I just know it," Brooke said.

"What, what, what?" Izzy spun in circles until she tumbled onto the ground.

Brooke giggled. "Be patient, you'll see."

"Remember, be careful what you wish for!" Calla said, pirouetting through the air.

Welcome to the
ENCHANTED PONY ACADEMY,
where dreams sparkle and magic shines!